The Fall of Castle Royale

M. Lindell & J. Lindell

DEDICATIONS

For every kid out there, remember that we do have the power to change things and make the world a better place.
~M. Lindell

For my boys, you have changed me for the better in more ways than you could ever possibly know. You've taught me to find my inner child and how to make life truly fun. May you never forget how amazing you make this world.
~J. Lindell

CONTENTS

ACKNOWLEDGMENT

We both would like to extend a very special 'thank you' to Scorpy, the artist who helped to illustrate this book. We supplied him with our ideas, and he turned them into the awesome graphics found within this book! If you would like to hire Scorpy for an illustration project, we highly recommend him. You can find him on Fiverr.com.

INTRODUCTION
WHAT'S THE BIG DEAL?!?

Before we get too deep, you might have noticed the title of this story. Why do I say that? Well, it seems that almost anything these days that has to do with Castle Royale grabs the attention of nearly half the human population.

What is Castle Royale you ask?

WHERE HAVE YOU BEEN?!?

If you are one of the rare few who has yet to learn of this wave crossing the planet, it is simply a video game.

But, one that is seemingly being played by every kid from K-12 and beyond. How I do know? Well, I'm pretty sure that my entire school plays it, because every time I ask my friends if they want to play other games, they look at me like I am completely insane.

What about Minecraft™? Nope. Call of Duty™? Nah. Madden™ or NBA2K™? Boo!

I just don't get it.

My friends don't even want to play Fortnite™ anymore, which makes no sense at all, because Castle Royale is basically the EXACT SAME GAME...with a different name.

I even try, with no luck, what used to be the go-to with most of my friends, pre-Castle Royale.

"Hey, you guys want to watch bad videos on YouTube?"

Not that I watch these videos on purpose, but have you been on YouTube lately? If you can find a video on your recommended page that isn't inappropriate, give me a call...better yet, give my Dad a call.

Anyway, all this leads me to believe that maybe Castle Royale is a conspiracy to take over the world.

Mayyyyybe?

More on that later...

CHAPTER 1
WHO DOESN'T PLAY CASTLE ROYALE?

Maybe it would help if you knew more about the ONE kid on the planet who has not been captured by this hysteria. That would be me. I'm Joey Baer. Yes, it's pronounced "bear," but if you start calling me Teddy, I'll lose it!

Other than my funny name, I think of myself as a pretty normal kid (however, disliking Castle Royale is anything BUT normal these days).

I am 10 years old, in fifth grade, go to school every day, and hang out with my friends. I enjoy video gaming, holidays (because it means days off from school), and any food that is absolutely terrible for me but tastes really great, AKA fast food, pizza and so on. Pretty normal, right? Put it to you this way. If the opposite of everything I just stated is normal, I don't want to live in that universe, except for the no school part. I could take that in any universe.

While feeling like I'm the only person in the world who hates Castle Royale is pretty discouraging, I am able to find some comfort when I get home from school each day. That leads me to my family.

My mom is great. She provides me with the great-tasting, terrible foods that I love. Wait, that came out the wrong way. She provides GOOD food that is terrible for me. NO. Uhhhh, let's just say she provides food for me.

She likes playing video games too, which is pretty cool for a Mom. She even has an actual Ocarina, which is a flute-like thing from the Zelda™ games, that she can actually play...not very well, but she tries. She usually has her hands full with my little brother, Bert.

Bert is a typical six-year old, who is learning how to read. He says funny things all the time. He is always there to cheer me up, when I have a bad day at school. So, that's cool. It's not all sunshine. He is a little bother, oh, I mean brother. He does get in the way sometimes, but it's cool to have a little brother. It's like having a personal assistant and a built-in opponent for bounce-house wrestling, who I can dominate like a boss. Don't worry too much about him; Bert holds his own and has won a couple of times.

His favorite video game of all time is Spiderman™. Sometimes it feels like he disappears for days on end, when I realize he's just locked himself away to play that game. I think he actually thinks he IS Spiderman™.

Then there is my Dad. This is where my feeling of after-school comfort truly comes in. You see, my Dad and I have quite a lot in common. Like me, he loves video games and often rage quits when they aren't going his way. Now that I think about it, that might be the only thing we have in common. BUT rage quitting IS an eternal bond.

If I'm being honest, I actually don't really know much about my Dad. I know he's old. Well, not super old, but older than me for sure. He tells me all the time that makes him smarter, which I can't confirm because I've never actually seen his report card. That said, he does have some higher level of intelligence, because, like me, he also hates Castle Royale.

I think this mostly has to do with the fact that I complain about it so much, and he HATES it when I complain. So, his hate of my complaining about Castle Royale, leads him to hate Castle Royale. All I know for sure is that when we both come home at the end of the day, only one of us needs to utter the words: "Castle Royale," and both of us are completely TRIGGERED! That is where my comfort comes from and is the one true, common bond that we share.

CHAPTER 2
FREEDOM OF CHOICE, EXERCISE IT!

As kids, we are living in a Golden Age of Video Games. How do I know this? Well, I have seen the games my parents used to play. Space Invaders™, Galaga™, Missile Command™. WHAT?! And, that's when games started to get cool.

My parents have even shown me videos of this "game" they loved called Pong™? If you don't know it, you HAVE to search it up. They play this game with paddles, instead of the high-tech controllers we are used to now. WHAT?! How about the original Nintendo™? Some of the games were good and still are. That is, if you played Super Mario Bros.™ or Donkey Kong™.

Today, we have Xbox™, Playstation™, PC gaming systems, virtual reality headsets, tablets and phones! We have access to literally thousands of games right at our fingertips 24 hours a day!

I can say there are probably 100 or more games that I actually like and could play right now.

Which leads me to the question:

Why would anyone settle on playing ONE game, every day, all the time, for hours on end?

Why would anyone JUST play **Castle Royale?**

ΔΔΔ

What's so good about it? The way I see it, it's basically a mash-up of Minecraft™ and every other shooter game out there. *"Oh, cool, I'm going to run around for hours on end and shoot people. Sweet, I can build a shelter for myself."* Right? This is what is capturing our imagination? Don't even get me started on the fact that every one of my guy friends wants to play as a girl character. I mean, my friends who are girls are fine. Some are great, actually. It's just that, well, what's wrong with being a guy? We're OK too, aren't we? I don't know, it's all very confusing.

This craze (or infection) over one stupid game actually makes me question society. I know. It might seem weird for a 10-year old to be questioning society, but this is where my Dad comes in. He is always saying how the world is going to "heck in a handbasket," in more entertaining words than I am allowed to state, of course.

Let's just say from this point forth "heck" will be used as a substitute for naughty words I hear my Dad saying from time to time. And, "heck in a handbasket?" I mentioned he was old, but that sounds really old-timey, even for him.

Sorry, I'm getting off topic here. Anyway, this Castle Royale craze makes me question some of my friends' choices.

Why settle on one game, all the time, when we have so many other options?

I've had some friends tell me they don't really like it but play because everyone else is. Ohhhhhh kayyyyyyy. (I can't do anything for you guys.) What about those who really DO like it? It has felt like everyone who plays games has been brainwashed except for me.

And then today happened and everything changed...

CHAPTER 3
THE STRANGE TRIANGLE

I head straight for the kitchen after school, so I can grab as many snacks as possible, before my mom interjects with the daily reminder, "Don't eat too much Joey, you'll ruin your dinner. Blah. Blah. Blah."

Sweet, no one is in there! I move like a ninja and grab some tortilla chips, a hunk of cheese, and a piece of candy left over from my Halloween haul. I don't want to go too crazy, so I opt for a glass of water over a juice box. (See, mom, I do listen.) I turn to head for the playroom, where I will feast on my snacks, and see my dad standing in the doorway, eyeing me suspiciously. Dad quickly inspects my haul, and apparently OK's it, because he doesn't motion for me to put anything back.

Phew, because I am really hungry. Fifth grade works up an appetite! I can't wait to consume it, so I grab a chip and start munching.

"Hey son, how was school today?" asks Dad.

I usually say the standard "OK," but not today. Today, I had enough of all of this Castle Royale stuff. Plus, I saw some weird things at school, so I decided to spill the beans.

"Mumm uhmss eemmaa, aaadd," I mumble excitedly in reply.

"Ex-squeeze me, son?" says my dad. He loves that 'ex-squeeze me' response. He literally giggles every time he says it. It's lame, but kinda dad-funny at the same it. "Don't talk with your mouth full. Swallow your food, take a sip of that water, and then let's try that again."

Thanks for the instructions on how to speak, Dad. I think I can handle this; I've been doing it for a while now. Defiantly, I follow his advice and take a huge gulp. OK, I'm ready.

"Actually, kind of weird, Dad," I reply.

"When I went to hand in my homework some other kids were handing in their assignments too. I noticed there was a strange triangle symbol at the top of their pages, on every single page," I continue.

"That's actually super good news son!" Dad exclaims, while grabbing one of my chips and starting to munch on it. "Mmmuubbeee Cccaastle Ruuulae," he stops takes a sip of my water and continues, "Maybe Castle Royale is done with and now everyone loves Zelda™, which is actually a good game!"

First of all, what actually? Did he just do what he told me not to do literally two seconds ago? Now, I'm a little annoyed, because I'm sharing something serious here and this guy is, well, being too dad. Maybe I need mom for this discussion. Where is she anyway? Think quickly---oh yeah, she's at Bert's karate class. They won't be home until dinner, so I guess I'm stuck with this guy.

"What the 'heck' are you talking about?" I shout.

Dad must realize the gravity of the situation, because he answers more seriously, "The triangle container. You know the thing in Zelda™, that gives Link all his powers. And, watch your language by the way!"

It baffles me sometimes that this man "plays" games. I decide to set him straight, "You mean

the Tri-Force! You really are a noob, Dad.
Maybe, you're just super old. You're nold."

Feeling quite proud of myself, I eat the rest of
my chips. Then I look up and notice that I struck
a nerve. OK, I didn't mean to hurt his
feelings. He is a cool dad. I mean, he's still
around to play Madden™ with, and he's always
up for a Smash Brothers™ challenge. I guess I
am being a bit harsh on the old man.

"Sorry, Dad, it was a good guess, but no, this
wasn't the Tri-Force," I say. "It was different.
There was like this eye thing in the middle of the
triangle. And, the really weird part was that I
noticed it in strange places all around the
school. It was in the library, the lunchroom, the
hallway, and even in the gym. What even?"

"Hmmmm, that is weird," Dad responds.
Clearly my apology had cooled him down. "Sorry
to hear it's not the Zelda™ thing. For a second, I
thought our dreams had come true. Anyway,
what the 'heck.' You should do an online search
and see if anything comes up."

ΔΔΔ

Normally, I wouldn't come right home from school and start doing Internet research. After six grueling hours in school, what kid wants to come home and do more work? YAY, fun! But, with all my friends playing Castle Royale, Dad out of ideas, and mom and Bert away until dinner, I didn't have anything better going on. Plus, the triangle symbol I saw at school today really is bothering me.

So, I wash my hands and put my dishes in the sink and head for the computer den. On my Dad's advice, I fire up the PC and get comfortable in the squishy office chair. I always feel like a boss when I sit in it. It's one of those big black executive chairs on wheels. I'm pretty sure I could figure out anything sitting in this chair. It's time to get to work. I open the search engine and type the word:

Triangle.

OK, that's a long list of results. Before I find myself venturing into a geometry lesson, I scroll back up to the top of the page to try again.

I type a more specific search term:

Triangle with eye.

I hit enter and one result comes up. Just one. Has this ever happened to you? Let me tell you it is weird; it is eerie in fact.

This is the result, "It All Exists and Revolves Around the Illuminati."

What? What the 'HECK' is Illuminati? It looks like it's from some other country. It's not even a .com address; it's at a .ill address? What the?

That's it; I'm totally weirded out here. I must be getting somewhere. I'm eager to get rid of this one result quickly, so I erase "triangle with an eye" and try to search for:

Illuminati.

No search results found.

Are you kidding me? Is someone watching me right now. How could this happen? No results? Is the Internet broken or something?

At this point, I am super-annoyed. If I were playing a video game, I would have rage-quit a long time ago, but I HAVE to figure this out.

So, for the 'heck' of it, let's search:

Castle Royale.

Of course, 18-gazillion pages come up. This is

exactly what I expect, and, of course, my computer freezes. What even? OK, let's reboot the computer and try this again.

I should have known that Castle Royale would break my computer too. It can't just ruin my game system, it has to find every ounce of technology in the house and compromise it. Ugh.

Waiting for my computer to restart, it hits me like a book thrown at me by my little brother! I need to search "Castle Royale Illuminati." I wait eagerly for the computer to go through all of its start-up functions. This, of course, is a good time to practice my office chair Olympics. I push off of the computer desk and whoosh myself across the room and pretend to hand someone a very important piece of paper. Then I whoosh myself back to the computer desk and hit it with a thud.

"Joey, what is going on in there?" my dad yells angrily from the other side of the house.

"Nothing, Dad," I yell back.

"Don't break anything in there; you sound like a herd of elephants!" he screams. I don't hear heavy footsteps coming my way, so I consider myself safe and get back to my work.

Awesome, the computer is ready. The next search I type is:

Castle Royale Illuminati. Enter.

Holy 'heck!' Only one page shows up again. Well, it's a picture, not a page. It's the picture I saw on everyone's papers today and all around the school, only it is bigger, so I can see it more clearly. It is a triangle with the words "Castle Royale" written in fancy lettering in the middle of the picture shaped like an eye.

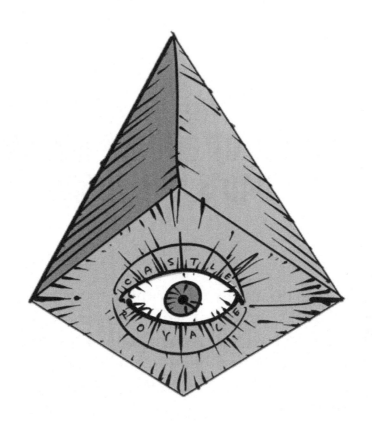

CHAPTER 4
EUREKA! PLOT UNCOVERED, AND MY DAD'S NOT DUMB!

This is definitely the graphic I saw today in school. Now, that I have an example, maybe Dad will recognize it. I quickly print the graphic and head to Dad's easy chair. After work, Dad usually heads for his chair to do some "reading," until Mom and Bert come home.

I storm into the room and excitedly say, "You won't believe this! The triangle has to do with something called the Illuminati and..."

"Dad sits up quickly in his chair, and says, "What? What!" His gaze fixed on me, as he continues, "Oh, I was just resting my eyes. What Joey? What did you find?"

"Dad, you won't believe this. That weird triangle I found all over school today has to do with something called the Illuminati," I reply. I show him the graphic I just printed.

"Oh yeah, I know them," Dad states, while adjusting himself and reaching for the paper to examine it.

"WHAT?" I scream taken aback.

"Yeah, they're supposedly like a New World Order, secret-society thing, that controls the entire world. No one really knows if they're real or not," Dad replies.

"This is interesting, Joe, it looks just like the Illuminati symbol, only with that game's title in the middle of it."

"Yeah, Dad, you think? YOU KNEW THIS AND THE FIRST THING THAT CAME TO YOUR MIND WAS THE TRI-FORCE!?!" I yell. Perhaps, the volume of my voice will indicate how upset this whole thing is making me.

Once again, a video game rage-quit would apply here to describe how fired up I am. I look up at my dad and his face looks disappointed again. I take a deep breath to calm myself down.

My mom always says, "You'll catch more flies with honey, sweetheart," meaning when you are nice, more people are willing to work with you. I really need my dad to work with me right now, so I temper my attitude and remember that he's trying to help.

I continue, "Dad, they are connected. The Illuminati and Castle Royale! Or, maybe..."

It hits me like that ice ball my brother threw at my back last winter. Cheap shot.

"The Illuminati IS Castle Royale!" I scream!

FINALLY, my Dad looks closely at the research I uncovered. Then I hover over his shoulder and look at it too. Just then, my Dad notices something that I missed.

"Son, there is a triangle symbol similar to this on the one-dollar bill," he says, reaching into his wallet and pulling out a bill that I could see for myself.

"Oh yeah, I see it," I say.

"And, look. There are three, dollar symbols on the triangle you found, in super tiny print," he says.

"I SEE THEM TOO!" I shout. "What the 'heck' does all of this mean?" I reply in a newly confused tone.

We're both speechless. Dad sits back in his easy chair, and I start pacing around the room. We both get into our thinking modes.

Dad is just sitting there, and time is passing so slowly it's killing me. I just look at him and wonder what's going on in that brain of his.

See, my dad's not an outward thinker. It makes me wonder how he was even able to get through school. When my class has to do something like a timed-math quiz, it's in moments like this where I picture Dad reading: "10 + 15 = __ " then sitting back in his chair, folding his arms behind his head, gazing up into the sky and pondering what the answer might be.

I suppose it's possible that he didn't finish school. Remember, I've never seen his report card. But there is some "wisdom" in him, which he tells me means he gets smarter with age. And, by now, we know he's old.

Why is this so hard to figure
out? Maybe, I should just forget the whole
thing and just go back to playing the
Splatoon 2™ campaign. Bored of staring a
hole through my father's head, I leave the
room and head toward the playroom.

As I make it into the hallway, he yells
for me to come back into the room.

It seemed to hit him like my mom the
day we got a new carpet, and he forgot to
take the dog out.

"Joey, I got it!" Dad yells.

"This is a simple but elaborate plot. The
Illuminati IS Castle Royale. Let's call
them the Digi-Nati."

"Dad, have you lost your mind?" I
reply. "Digi-Nati is the name of the
company that makes Castle
Royale. Hahaha. You didn't just make
that up."

"It is?" Dad asks genuinely surprised
that he didn't just come up with that name
out of nowhere.

"Yeah, Dad, Digi-Nati, the makers of Castle Royale. It's all over Twitch and YouTube. Please don't make me call you a noob again. What's the rest of your theory," I say.

Dad shakes his head, as if I just flipped his world upside down.

"Well, maybe they have these symbols all over your school as mind-control devices to get the kids to play the game non-stop," he says reluctantly.

"You mean like advertising?" I ask.

"No, Joey, maybe this is a bit more controlling than advertising. Maybe there is something in these symbols that subliminally persuades kids to play the game," says Dad.

"OK, dad, assuming all of that is true, why would they want to do that, AND how could a little symbol on a paper subliminally persuade anyone to do anything? It seems a bit far-fetched," I say. "I mean, why would the Digi-Nati want kids to play this dumb game so much?"

Dad leans back in his recliner, smiles

and says, "Easy, Joe. Money. The answer is money." Dad suddenly sits up and says, "The more kids they can get to play the game, the more money they bring in. Think about it. If these symbols are in other schools, which they probably are since we know that Castle Royale is a world-wide craze, then think about how much money the Digi-Nati can make. The dollar amount is staggering!"

"Endless money means endless power. The Digi-Nati could control the world with a never-ending cash supply. They could buy what they want, influence who they want, do whatever they want, and no one in the general public is aware of it. Most adults are too busy trying to keep their homes functioning to worry deeply about the video games their children are playing. Using kids to generate income for a secret organization is just plain smart. Unethical? Yes, but it's also really smart," he concludes.

   With that, I am truly speechless. My
head is swimming with all of the
information my dad just shared with
me. Could he be right? Is the Digi-Nati
using kids to generate income for a secret
society that plans to rule the world? It's a
lot to take in.

   Maybe my dad made it through school
after all. I don't know, maybe not, but I
now know that he isn't an idiot. He should
get up from that easy chair more often.

CHAPTER 5
THE ROOT OF ALL EVIL...
AND CASTLE ROYALE!

Everything is finally coming together. I take a couple of minutes to toss these ideas around, and then I share my thoughts with Dad.

"Dad, that makes perfect sense!" I state. "But, couldn't they just make money by selling the game without secretly brainwashing people?"

Dad replies, "What? No! You've said it yourself a million times that the game stinks, so why would anybody buy and play a cruddy game unless they were brainwashed into it?"

He has a point. Now this makes PERFECT sense to me.

"So, the Digi-Nati's ultimate goal is to get super rich?" I ask. "That seems like a pretty dumb reason to brainwash kids."

Dad responds, "I don't know, son. Money is pretty sweet, and there are a lot of greedy people in the world. Personally, I don't think it would be too bad to win the lottery and be able to swim in a pool full of coins."

"Dad, you can't swim in coins. You can make it rain dollar bills, but a pool full of coins would be pointless. You couldn't move at all in it. You could get a gold-plated pool and countless other practical additions for the house though," I say snapping him back into the moment.

So, what my Dad and I finally figured was that this whole Digi-nati thing all really boils down to making a ton of money. Which is just fine. Who doesn't want to have a ton of money? Except for the fact that Castle Royale stinks. Because of that, I would say on principle alone this plot must be stopped!

But there's more to it than just principle, and it goes back to what I said before. If all these kids knew what they were missing out on. There are so many other fun and fulfilling games. Ones that challenge our gaming skills, open our minds and expand our imaginations. Games that allow us to experience all that life has to offer through great quests, side missions and storytelling, instead of just the same ole thing over and over and over.

I wish everyone could see things the way I do.

CHAPTER 6
MY "OBVIOUS" IMMUNITY

After discovering this world-wide conspiracy, the only other thing for us to do was to figure out how to stop it. As my Dad and I brainstormed ideas, I found myself slipping into a daydream...

(Oh, how great it will be to freely play any and all video games again without Castle Royale-shaming... Oh, how great it will be to actually have friends to play online with again... Oh, how I'm gonna smash my little brother later for accidentally deleting my favorite iPad app... Stay on task...)

Sorry, I'm back. I realize I am staring into the sky with my arms folded behind my head. Maybe I do have some things in common with my Dad after all.

It seemed like hours that we sat around trying to figure out ideas.

Then my Dad says simply, "Son, you don't like Castle Royale."

"Well, DUH. Captain Obvious," I respond.

"No, think about it," he continues. "Why does every other kid like it and you don't? How come the symbols haven't brainwashed you?"

Well, DUH is right. How come I haven't been affected by the symbols. The answer has been right in front of us all along...well, right in front of my Dad if I was standing in front of him... and, right in front of me, if I was looking in a mirror. You get the point.

Anyway, I was somehow immune to the brainwash power of these symbols. But how? I didn't know for sure, but it sounded like it was going to call for more research, AKA more work. Yay.

"I've got an idea, but we need to get in front of one of these symbols at your school," says Dad. "Seems like we need to take a field trip."

Oh no. is this what I think it means...

My Dad continues, "I think there is a basketball game at the school tonight, so we should be able to get in without any problems. We will find one of these symbols and do an experiment."

Great! Just what I thought. A field trip... TO SCHOOL! Awesome! What could be better than spending all day in school, then going back at night?! Meh. Well, if it meant finding answers, I guess I can endure.

CHAPTER 7
THE POWER OF MANY GAMES

We arrive at school later that evening. As Dad thought, we are able to walk right in because of the basketball game being played. Well, my Dad did have to pay admission, which he wasn't exactly pleased with. Let's just say his facial expression looked like it does when I call him a noob.

We spent some time searching the hallways, where I have noticed the symbols. It didn't take us long to find the first one.

"OK, stand in front of it and stare at it," says Dad.

I have to admit, I am a bit scared, but we need to figure this out.

"OK, here it goes..." I reply nervously.

I walk right up to the symbol, face forward, but can't (or won't) open my eyes.

"What's wrong son," asks Dad.

"What if...what if I open my eyes, look at this symbol and start to love Castle Royale?" I say stammering. "What if I haven't been brainwashed because I just haven't looked hard enough before? What if I become like everyone else and all I want to play is that game?"

My Dad pauses for what seemed to be a long while.

He takes a deep breath and says, "That's the chance you're going to have to take. Besides, if I ever caught you playing that game, I would smash the Xbox, so you'd never have to worry about playing it again."

"Ohhhhhh kayyyyy. That's comforting...I guess," I reply. "Alright, I'm doing it."

I slowly open my eyes and stare right at the triangle symbol.

Nothing.

Just then, I blink my eyes and see a flash of light. But, in the flash I see a different symbol. With my first blink...

I see a Minecraft diamond block.

The second blink...

An EA sports logo.

The third...

Mario looking right back at me.

The fourth...

A triangle of...the Tri-Force. I guess Dad planted that seed.

The point is, with every blink, I see a different symbol from just about every different video game I play. I tell my Dad what I'm experiencing and everything that I see.

"It makes total sense," says Dad. "You have spent so many hours playing so many different video games, the Digi-nati symbol has no power over you. You love so many games, one game alone can't take over your mind. Every other kid that sees these symbols, must be seeing only Castle Royale images over and over again."

From there, we spend another hour searching the school for as many Digi-nati symbols as we can find. Just to be sure, I perform the exact same experiment in front of all of symbols we find, with the same result.

NOW we are getting somewhere. As we exit the school to head home, I note something very important to my Dad

"Dad?" I ask. "Yes, son?" He answers.

I ask with a hopeful optimism, "Since I spent two extra hours at school today, can I go in two hours late tomorrow morning?"

Uh oh, the noob-face again. I'll take that as a 'no.' It doesn't matter anyway, because I am filled with an energy I haven't felt in a long time. We are close! With what we discovered, it seems like there is a way to end this Castle Royale hysteria once and for all and diffuse the power of those Digi-nati symbols. It's just going to mean getting kids to realize there's so much more out there to experience, instead of just this one game.

Wait, that doesn't sound easy at all. How is one kid going to reach the entire world? How can I convince all the other kids in the world to open their minds to all gaming possibilities? There has to be a way to reach out.

But how?

CHAPTER 8
WHERE THERE'S CLICKBAIT, THERE'S A WAY

My excitement over the discovery my Dad and I had made at the school that one night, quickly faded. Two weeks have passed, and I have no idea how to reach every kid across the planet with one simple message. My Dad is stumped too. We are both so discouraged, we are thinking about giving up and giving in. Castle Royale will go on forever.

As I often do when I am feeling down, I pull up a few of my favorite YouTube channels to get a laugh. As I'm watching one of my favorite YouTubers, I realize the description of his video:

"******EXCLUSIVE FIRST LOOK AT THE LOST LEVELS. YOU WILL ONLY FIND THIS HERE*********"

As I'm watching the video, I start to realize that these 'lost levels' aren't even in the video, and that the YouTuber doesn't even mention them. I then realized that the video has about 1 million views.

So, he has a super-fake title that gets everyone to tune into his video, no matter what the actual video is about. Seems pretty dishonest.

But, hey, if it works. IT WORKS!

It all starts to come together!

I spend what seems like hours every day watching videos on the very outlet that is my answer: A YouTube video message! This is how I can reach the world in one shot.

Super-excited again, I run into my Dad's home office to tell him my idea.

"One, single YouTube message, broadcast to every kid in the world! That's the way!" I scream.

"The way to what?" Dad replies confused.

I was wrong, he is an idiot.

"You know!" I yell. "To tell them of the
Digi-nati plot and to open their minds to
the possibilities of other games. DID YOU
FORGET WHAT WE'VE BEEN DOING
ALL THIS TIME?!"

"Oh, oh yeah! That does make sense.
Actually, that's a super good idea!" Dad
responds.

Finally! He has come back to life,
everybody!

"Right!" I continue. "Every kid I know watches YouTube. Especially, the channels and videos that have to do with games. AND, I know exactly what we have to do to make sure every kid tunes in."

"What's that, son?" Dad questions.

"Clickbait!" I exclaim. "But, not just any clickbait. The most super-epic clickbait ever created. So epic that no human being alive will be able to take their eyes off the screen without watching the video."

Dad asks, "Soooo, you're basically going to brainwash kids into watching your video so that they can stop being brainwashed by the Digi-nati?"

"Well, I wouldn't call it brainwashing exactly." I reply. "It's more like good advertising. Right?"

"Sure, let's say that. Whatever works," Dad concludes.

CHAPTER 9
THE EPIC APPEAL

We have our plan. Now, we need to make it work. My Dad has a video-editing background from an old job he used to have so he can do what is needed to get the message uploaded. So, we just need a message. Dad takes care of that. Or, tries to. He hands me a script.

"Just read this when you get on camera," he says.

I start reading it to myself.

"Kids of the world. You are being brainwashed. Wake up. Castle Royale stinks. Other games are better..."

Holy 'heck' this is awful! It is now an absolute certainty. He is a complete and utter idiot.

"Uhhhhhh, Dad?" I say.

"Yes?" he responds.

"How about we just ditch the script, and I speak from the heart?" I say.

"You sure?" he asks.

"POSITIVE." I add.

"Ok, it is your video. Just hang on to the script though, in case you need it. There is some really good stuff in there," he finishes.

I agree, if 'really good stuff' means complete trash. We setup a video camera and simply put a chair in front of it. No backdrop needed. Dad said he could edit one in and put logos and symbols from other games in the background of the video. The rest is up to me. So, I sit in front of the camera.

What should I say?

Then I remember to just speak from the heart...

So, I look at the camera and start to speak.

"What if I told you that you are not free? You are being told over and over that you are free to make your own choices, but it just isn't true. You are being controlled and what's even scarier is how it is happening.

Hello world! I'm Joey Baer. Like all of

you, I am just a normal, average, everyday kid, who LOVES to play video games. I not only love to play campaigns and solo missions, but I also LOVE to connect with my friends and play online challenges. But, about a year ago, my friends stopped playing the games we all liked, and they started playing CASTLE ROYALE. Ugh.

At first, there was no big deal about the switch, because new games come out all the time and kids try them out. However, I quickly noticed something different about Castle Royale. My friends were leaving, and they weren't coming back to play any other games they used to love. I'm an avid gamer who is always ready for a new challenge, so I tried Castle Royale too, but I never got into it. I couldn't figure out where the true challenge was. I mean, there's no real storyline. We've all seen the FPS games before. Wow, you can build some structures in this game. OK. We've seen that in Minecraft. What's the deal? The game is OK, but it's not worthy of mass hysteria. Not even close.

So, for a long time, I just gave up. I played my games by myself and really haven't thought much about multiplayer gaming for a long time. That was until last week. You are NOT going to believe me. Heck, I wouldn't believe me, but I have to get this message out. Literally, YOUR FREEDOM depends on this story getting out. If you play Castle Royale, YOU really need to hear this message. The makers of Castle Royale are brainwashing you. I know; it sounds impossible, maybe even a bit silly. But, it's true. Have you seen the funky triangles that are showing up everywhere? Think hard.

They look like this.

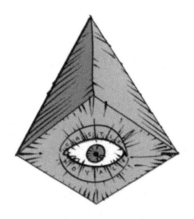

It's is the stamp of the Digi-nati. All of the places you see that symbol, Castle Royale's creators, or Digi-nati, have seized control of them. The more you see those symbols, the more you want to play. So, you might be thinking, who cares?

Well, I for one care. Why do they need

to control you? To make money, of
course. In the land of grownups, money
equals power. Have you ever begged your
parents for CR-Bucks? Duh, of course, you
have. We, kids, are spending tons of REAL
money inside a game that's not really
giving us anything.

The Digi-nati are taking ours and our
parents' hard-earned real money, and they
are using it to try and control the
WORLD! I for one do not want to live in
that world. I like the freedom to play the
games I want to play.

So, let me finish by asking you all one
simple question.

*Why spend all of your precious free time
and energy playing one video game?*

It's a game where you simply run around
for hours on end and shoot at other
characters doing the exact same thing,
with no end point, no less.

Why do this, when you can be building
epic castles in Minecraft™ or forming
mountains in LEGO Worlds™, where the
only limit is your imagination? When you
can be exploring the vast universes of
Skyrim™ or Destiny™? When you can be

teaming up with your best friends to win world championships in Madden™ or NBA2K™? When you can clan up with those same best friends and dominate in Call of Duty™ or Battlefield™? When you can be having a good ole fashion smackdown in Smash Bros™, Mortal Kombat™ or Streetfighter™? Or, when you can consume the great storylines and gameplay of Halo™, Final Fantasy™ or the entire Legend of Zelda™ series???

There are so many awesome, entertaining and fulfilling games in my head right now, to list them all would take hours! And, with many of these games, you don't even need to purchase in-game content to continue enjoying them. The experience of these games is the enjoyment, not some crazy new character skin that adds nothing to the gameplay.

So, I leave you with one final request.

*Fall in love with **ALL** video games again, not just **ONE** video game.*

That doesn't mean that we can't have a favorite video game, but let's not forget about the other games that fill our minds and hearts with an endless supply of fun and entertaining experiences. So, when you turn this video off, go find a game you used to love to play. Put that game in your console and start to remember why you loved it to begin with. Then each day do the same thing with another game you haven't played in a while, until you fall in love with all games again. Then, we can all truly call ourselves free gamers.

Thank you for listening and happy gaming to you all...Oh, and sorry about the title of the video. I'll admit, clickbait is the WORST!"

ΔΔΔ

I look at Dad and ask, "Well?"

He is looking away. Then, he slowly turns and looks at me. HE HAS TEARS IN HIS EYES! Next thing I know he walks right over to me, stands up straight, then salutes me, like I'm a general or something. Then, as customary whenever I do something that he is super proud of, he grabs my hand and shakes it.

See, Dad's not a hugger so this is how he shows affection through good, firm handshakes.

"Soooo, it was OK?" I ask again.

"Solid gold, son. If that doesn't reach people, nothing will," my Dad replies, his voice quivering.

Now, just add a title and get it uploaded. But not just any title. Remember?

The most super-epic clickbait ever:

**** NEW ****** CASTLE ROYALE EXCLUSIVE ******* ONLY HERE FIRST, WOW, OMG ****** EPIC SNIPER PACKAGE, WITH MAGIC TRAVELING BULLET ********* SHOOT ACROSS ENTIRE MAP ******** FIRST 100 to LIKE ******* GET 15 NEW GIRL SKINS, NEVER BEFORE SEEN *****

I think that might work. There's only one way to find out...

CHAPTER 10
DID IT WORK?

Dad took my message and did his video editing magic. He added some logos and images from games I mentioned, added our clickbait, and uploaded it all to YouTube.

"Now what?" I ask.

Dad responds, "I guess we wait."

"But what if nobody watches it?" I ask again. "Or what if kids watch it, and it doesn't work?"

"Well, I guess nothing changes, and you and I stay miserable. But at least we will have each other!" Dad finishes.

With that, I shut the computer down and walk away. I am not interested in refreshing the video message over and over again, to see if anybody is liking it, let alone viewing it. I can't take the disappointment if it isn't reaching anyone. So, I plan to just go on as I do every day.

ΔΔΔ

When I got back to school the next day. Tons of kids came up to me to tell me they had seen my video. Some of them thought it was funny. Some said they really liked it. Others were completely TRIGGERED because of the clickbait. Well, at least that worked. But, other than that, it didn't seem to really change anything. Then, over the course of the day I started to notice some things. I saw a kid with his Nintendo DS playing Super Smash Bros™.

Later, I saw a friend of mine in study hall reading a Minecraft™ guide on epic, castle construction. And, on the bus ride home, a kid was playing a Call of Duty™ app on his iPad™. Promising signs? Maybe I did reach people? I guess time will tell.

EPILOGUE
3 MONTHS LATER

It's Friday afternoon, every kids' favorite school day! Especially considering the clock had one minute until the 3 p.m. dismissal bell.

In 3... 2... 1... I'm outta this place and off for the weekend to play VIDEO GAMES! ...and, chores... (I'll let my parents think that those are on the top of my priority list. HA! So my parents think.)

DING! DING! DING! DING! DING! The bell sounds and everyone hops off their seats and heads for the lockers. As I'm walking to the school bus, a couple of my good friends come over to me.

"Hey, man, we gaming tonight?" they ask.

I reply "You know it, guys! What are we playing?"

"I don't know. We can figure it out later. The options are endless!" they say together.

I conclude, "How about we just say, anything but **Castle Royale**."

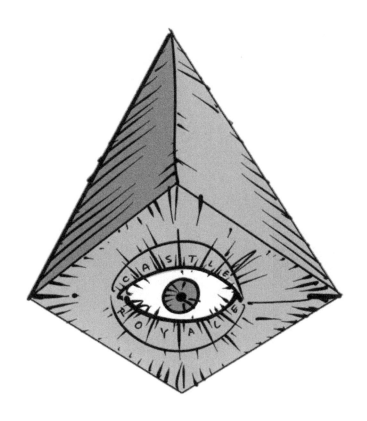

THE END???

ABOUT THE AUTHORS

M. LINDELL

M. Lindell loves video games of all genres. He especially likes connecting with friends online and exploring the vast environments new gaming experiences offer. He attends school in New York, and he lives with his brother, mother, father, and best fur-friends, Sadie (the family's golden retriever) and Charlotte (the family's newest puppy addition).

J. LINDELL

J. Lindell has always had a love for all things videos games, from his childhood, to gaming with his kids, as an adult. He is passionate about life-long learning and helping his kids become the best human beings they can be. J. lives in New York with his two children and his wife.

Made in the USA
Middletown, DE
09 December 2020